First published in the United States, Great Britain, Canada, Australia, and New Zealand in 2014
by NorthSouth Books Inc., an imprint of NordSüd Verlag AG, CH-8005 Zürich, Switzerland.

Distributed in the United States by NorthSouth Books Inc., New York 10016.

Library of Congress Cataloging-in-Publication Data is available.
ISBN: 978-0-7358-4172-7
1 3 5 7 9 • 10 8 6 4 2
Printed in Germany by Grafisches Centrum Cuno
GmbH & Co. KG, Calbe, January 2014.

www.northsouth.com

The
SIX SWANS

THE BROTHERS GRIMM · *illustrated by* GERDA RAIDT

translated by ANTHEA BELL

North South

Once upon a time a king went hunting in a great forest. He chased a deer, and went so fast that none of his followers could keep up. When evening came he stopped and looked around him, and saw that he had lost his way. He searched for a path leading out of the forest, but he could not find one. Then he saw an old woman with a wagging head coming through the trees. However, this old woman was really a witch.

"Good woman," said the king, "can you show me the way out of this forest?"

"Yes, Your Majesty," said the witch. "Indeed I can, but on one condition, and if you do not agree to do as I ask, you will never get out of the forest but die here of starvation."

"What is the condition?" asked the king.

"I have a daughter," said the old witch. "She is the most beautiful girl in the world and worthy to be your wife. Make her your queen, and I will show you the way out of the forest."

In his great fear the king agreed, and the old woman led him to her little house, where her daughter was sitting by the fire.

The witch's daughter welcomed the king as if she had been expecting him, and he saw that she was indeed very beautiful. Yet he did not like her and could not look at her without a secret sense of horror.

When he had lifted the girl up to sit on his horse with him, the old woman showed him the way to go, and the king returned to his royal castle, where the wedding was celebrated.

Now, the king had been married before, and his first wife had borne him six sons and one daughter, whom he loved more than anything in the world. Fearing that their stepmother might not treat them well, he took them to live in a lonely castle in the middle of a forest. It was so well hidden away, and the path was so difficult to find, that he could not have made his own way there if a wise woman had not given him a magic ball of string. When he threw the ball ahead of him, it unwound by itself and guided him through the forest.

The king went to visit his dear children so often that the new queen noticed his frequent absences. She was curious, and wondered what he could be doing out in the forest all alone. So she bribed his servants with a great deal of money to give the secret away. They also told her about the ball of string, the only way of finding the castle.

The queen would not rest until she had discovered where the king kept the ball of string. Then she made some little shirts of white silk and sewed a magic spell that she had learned from her mother into each shirt.

One day when the king was hunting, she took the little shirts out into the forest, and the ball of string showed her the way.

Seeing someone in the distance, the king's sons thought their dear father was coming to see them. They were delighted and ran to meet him. Then the queen threw a shirt over each of them, and as soon as the shirts touched them they turned into swans and flew away over the forest.

The queen went home satisfied, believing she was rid of her stepchildren. But the girl had not come running with her brothers, and the queen did not even know she existed.

The next day the king went to see his children, but he found no one in their castle except the girl.

"Where are your brothers?" asked the king.

"Oh, dear Father," she replied, "they've gone away and left me all alone!"

Then she told her father how she had been watching from her window when her brothers flew away over the forest in the shape of swans, and she showed him a few feathers. They had fallen in the castle courtyard, and she had picked them up.

The king was very sad, but he never guessed that his queen had done this dreadful thing. Fearing to lose his daughter too, he would take her home with him.

But she was afraid of her stepmother and asked the king to let her stay in the castle in the forest for just one more night.

When night came, she escaped from the castle and went straight into the forest to search for her brothers. She walked and walked, all night and all the next day, until she felt so tired that she could go no farther.

Then she saw a hunting lodge. She went in and found a room with six little beds. Not daring to get into one of the beds, she crawled underneath one instead and lay down on the hard floor, meaning to spend the night there.

However, just as the sun was about to sink, she heard a rushing noise and saw six swans come flying in the window. They all settled on the floor and blew at one another until they had blown all their feathers away, and their swans' skins came off too, like shirts.

The girl, watching, was overjoyed to recognize her brothers, and she came out from under the bed.

Her brothers were equally delighted to see their sister, but their joy did not last long.

"You can't stay here," they told the girl. "This is a robbers' den, and if those thieves come home and find you, they'll kill you."

"Can't you protect me?" asked their sister.

"No," said the brothers, "for we may shed our feathers and return to human shape for only a quarter of an hour every evening, and then we turn back into swans again."

"Is there no way I can save you?" asked their sister, weeping.

"Oh, no," they said, "the conditions are too hard. To save us, you must not say a word for six long years, or laugh, either, and in that time you must sew us six shirts made of starflowers. And if a single word escapes your lips, all your work will be wasted."

As soon as the brothers had told her this, the quarter of an hour came to an end, and they flew out the window again in the shape of swans.

The girl made up her mind that she would save her brothers even at the cost of her life. She left the hunting lodge, went out into the forest, and climbed a tree, where she spent the night.

The next morning she gathered starflowers, and then she began sewing. There was no one for her to talk to, and she did not feel at all like laughing. She sat sewing day after day, with eyes for nothing but her work.

When she had been living in the forest for some time, it so happened that the king of that country went hunting in the forest, and his huntsmen saw the tree where the girl was sitting. They called up to her, "Who are you?" But she did not reply.

"Come down," said the huntsmen. "We won't hurt you."

She merely shook her head, and when they asked more questions, she threw her gold necklace down, hoping they would be content with that.

But they still asked questions, so she threw down her belt; and when that did not satisfy them either, she threw down her garters, and then all the clothes she was wearing one by one, until she could spare no more and was left in nothing but her shift. Still the huntsmen would not go away. They climbed the tree, brought the girl down, and took her to the king.

"Who are you?" asked the king, "and what were you doing in that tree?" The girl did not answer, and the king repeated his question in every language he knew; but she remained as mute as a fish. She was so beautiful that the king's heart was touched, and he fell in love with her. He put his cloak around her, lifted her up to sit on his horse, and took her to his castle, where he had her dressed in rich clothes. In her finery, she was as beautiful as the day, but still she would not utter a word.

He made her sit beside him at dinner, and her modesty and good manners pleased him so much that he said, "I will marry no one in the world but this girl." So a few days later their wedding was held.

But the king had a wicked mother who did not like the marriage and spread slander about the young queen.

"Who knows where the girl comes from?" she said. "She can't even speak; she is no wife for a king."

A year later, when the queen had a baby, the old woman stole it away. Then she went to the king and told him his wife had disposed of their child.

The king refused to believe it and would not let anyone hurt his wife. The queen herself still sat sewing her shirts and paid no attention to anything else.

Some time later she had another fine baby, and her wicked mother-in-law played the same trick, but still the king could not bring himself to believe what the old woman said. "My wife is too good and gentle to be capable of such a thing," he said. "If she were not mute and could defend herself, her innocence would be plain to everyone."

But the third time that the old woman stole the newborn baby and accused the queen of killing it, and the queen said not a word to defend herself, the king saw that there was no help for it. He must let his wife be tried for murdering her children, and she was condemned to be burned at the stake.

The queen's execution was set for the very day that marked the end of the six years when she must not speak or laugh. The six shirts were finished, all except the last, which still had no left sleeve. She had freed her dear brothers from the power of the magic spell.

When the queen was brought out to be burned, she had the shirts over her arm, and as she stood by the stake and the fire was about to be kindled, she looked around her. Then six swans came flying through the air. She saw that she would be saved, and her heart leapt for joy. The swans flew to her and came down lower so that she could throw the shirts over them . . .

and when the shirts touched the swans, their feathers fell away, and there stood her own brothers before her, handsome and well, except that the youngest had a swan's wing growing from his back instead of a left arm. They all embraced and kissed, and the queen went to the king, who was watching in amazement.

"Dearest husband," she said, "now at last I can speak and tell you I was falsely accused, and I am innocent." Then she told him how the wicked old woman had stolen her three children and hidden them away.

To the king's great delight, his children were found and brought to him, and as a punishment the queen's wicked mother-in-law was taken away and locked up forever.

But the king and queen, and the queen's six brothers, lived for many years in peace and happiness.

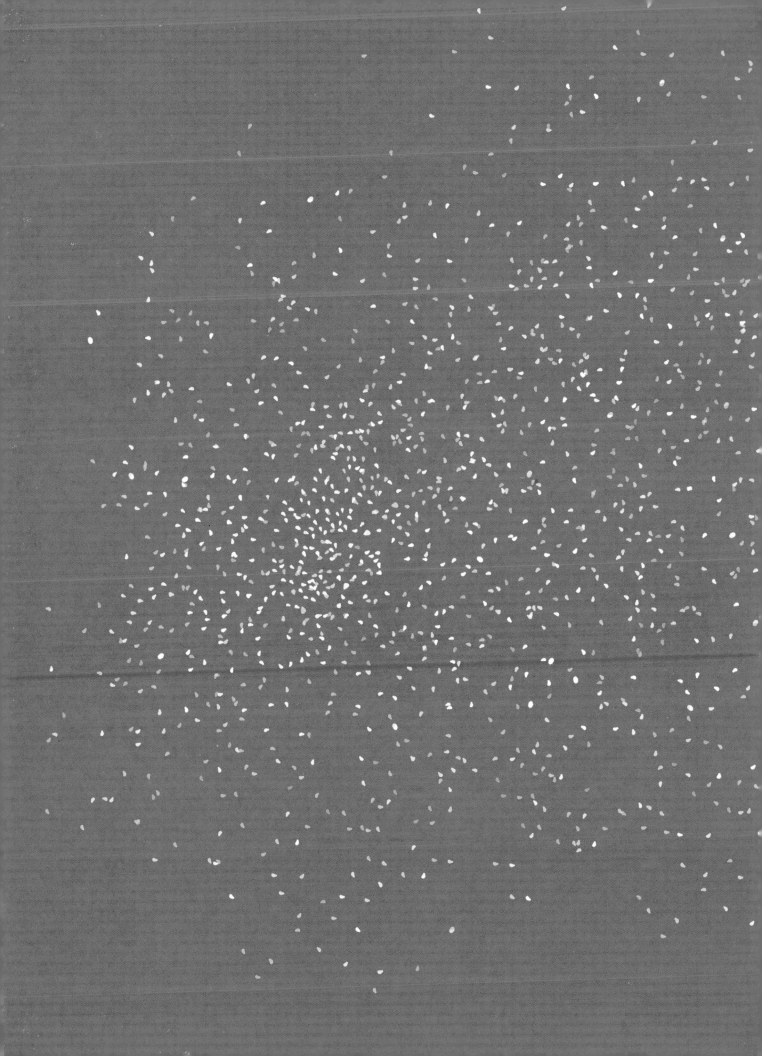